That's Not  Fair!

Written by Heather Gemmen
Illustrated by Luciano Lagares

www.cookcommunications.com/kidz

A Faith Parenting Guide can be found at the back of book.

I hug myself in pure delight
At such a perfect end.

The shoe fits Cinderella well!
She'll never clean again.

3

Miss Betsy asks us what we like
About the book she read.

I sit up straight and raise my hand;
My eyes look straight ahead.

I didn't blurt or wave my hand—
And that's why she picked me.

"I love it when the bad guys lose
And good guys are set free."

"That's right," my teacher said to me.
"We like things to be fair.
Aren't you glad that God is just?"
She hugged me from her chair. . .

I'll be good forever now.
It makes Miss Betsy glad.

I'll always try to make things fair.
I never will be bad.

Miss Betsy's busy helping Tim
When Kelly grabs a toy.

"That's not fair!" I shout at her.
"She's being mean to Troy!"

Kelly had to do time-out,
And Troy gave me a smile.

I'm glad that things are all cleared up—
At least a little while.

When it's time to cut and glue
Cassandra just won't share.

"Miss Betsy!" I yell out to her.
"She's not being fair!"

The teacher comes to sit with us.
She helps us cut and glue.
Cassandra has to share her stuff.
Miss Betsy told her to.

I like it that I have a job
That helps my teacher out.

Whenever something isn't right
I give her a quick shout.

At recess time Miss Betsy asks
If I will stay inside.

But when I hear her awful words,
I just want to hide.

"You can't tell on other kids
for everything they do.

I plug my ears and start to stomp.
(I know that it's not right.)
My teacher pulls me in her arms
And hugs me warm and tight.

"There's good and bad in all of us,"
She whispers in my ear.
"We all are precious as we are."
She wipes away my fear.

I'm glad that God will teach us when
We do things that are wrong.

I'm glad that he forgives us soon.
God's love is very strong.

That's Not Fair!

Life Issue: I want my children to quit tattling.

Spiritual Building Block: Grace

Help your children to understand God's grace and justice in the following ways:

Sight: Wake your children early one morning to snuggle under a blanket to watch the sunrise. As you watch, talk about how God made a plan that causes the sun to rise and set in a regular pattern. We like things to be orderly and consistent, too. We have to balance that desire with the need for grace. God's sunrise is orderly and beautiful.

Sound: Find a child-friendly version of the Bible, and read Hosea 11 to your children. Help them to understand how much God loves us, how sad he becomes because of our sin, and how deeply he wants to forgive us. Explain to them that God agrees with our desire for fairness, but he also wants us to forgive.

Touch: Next time one of your children tattles on another, take both children by the hand and lead them to a quiet place. Ask the child who has tattled to help the child who has done wrong to make a better choice. Your role is only to monitor the conversation; encourage the kids to find a healthy solution to the situation by themselves.